ZIGGY ZEBRA

by S.L. Danziger

Zebra goes to a normal school full of normal elephants and normal kangaroos, they don't understand Zebra though because they don't understand what they don't know.

Zebra paints his face like his favorite rock star and pretends to go fast in his cardboard sports car.

One day Bully Bear came up to Zebra, bent down his head and glared as he said, "You're weird Zebra, you're not like us, you paint your face and you ride the bus."

Zebra looked up and in barely a whisper, he stood up to the bear with not even a quiver.

"I'm not weird you see for I'm just me, I'm Ziggy Zebra and that's all I can be."

"You're not Ziggy Zebra, I know who he is, you just pretend and paint your face like his. You're not he, he's on T.V., you're just a zebra and that's all you'll ever be."

Zebra just turned and he went on his way for he felt so sad and didn't know what to say. Maybe I am weird, he said to himself, I know who can help me, wise Grandfather Birdelf!

Grandfather Birdelf was a wise man you see, he lived in a tree filled with birds and with bees. He sat in his chair and he sipped on his tea, he nodded his head and listened patiently.

Finally when he was ready to speak, the wise words just tumbled right out of his beak, "Dare to be different, don't try to fit in. You'll find your kind one day, I promise my friend."

Zebra forced a smile and he went on his way, he tried to understand what Grandfather did say.

But I want to fit in, he thought as he marched, I'll take off my paint and I'll have a fresh start!

No sooner than the thoughts had entered his mind, he looked up to the field, "Oh my, my own kind!"

There dancing and prancing in the field being free were Ziggy Mouse, Ziggy Fox and Ziggy the bee. There were Ziggy fish and dogs, Ziggy cats and hogs, they were all there being hearty at Ziggy Zebra's big party!

Zebra laughed and he danced, he twirled and he pranced. He learned a valuable lesson that day, that being yourself is the only way.

Many years down the road when the kids were all grown, Zebra was a rock star all on his own. At one of his shows standing in the front row, he saw Bully Bear and his heart began to glow, for he had forgiven those who once were not nice, other bullies, he thought might now think twice.

There once was a monkey named Shain and she was the happiest monkey you ever did see. She painted zebras and danced under stars, she smiled and waved at all passing cars. She rolled in the grass and she sang to the trees, she made bubble baths just to wash her knees!

One day it was raining and Teacher said, "No playing outside Shain, you must stay in instead." Shain was very sad but only for a tad for she couldn't sit and pout while Teacher had so many fun things out!

Teacher had all sorts of games to play like make believe princesses, cops and robbers and charades! Shain made puppets out of socks and painted flowers onto rocks. She made necklaces out of macaroni and invented an instrument called the Zamboni!

Before Shain knew it, it was time to go home and she sadly put down her crown.

"I hope tomorrow is another rainy day, I have more things to invent and more games to play!"

Sometimes it will rain, sometimes it will be grey, sometimes things simply won't go your way. Continue to smile and laugh and be gay, if you make the most of things, you can always play.

THE SUN

One day the sun woke up and she said, "I don't want to be the sun anymore, I want to be the moon instead!"

She turned off her lights and went totally dark, her surfaced iced over and left not even a spark.

On earth it had been a warm, sunny day, the children had all been outside at play. Whatever they were doing, they all had to go in because the earth became so very cold and so incredibly dim.

The kids started to cry as they hugged their friends goodbye. They didn't understand why Sun would do such a thing for in their minds, she reigned supreme.

Sun woke quickly to the children's cries, she woke with quite the start. She quickly dressed, she put on her best, and she ran to relight her spark.

I'm needed, she smiled and laughed to herself, I'll never try to be anyone else. I'll never again want to be the moon or the stars or anything other than myself.

NIKKI

Nikki the bird wanted to fly, she desperately wanted to touch the sky. Try as she could and try as she might, Nikki the bird simply couldn't take flight. Up she soared then down she went for Nikki the bird, well she was spent!

She came through the door and she started to cry, she hugged Mama Bird and said, "I don't care if I fly!" But care she did, she couldn't pretend, Mama Bird knew, she had been through it too.

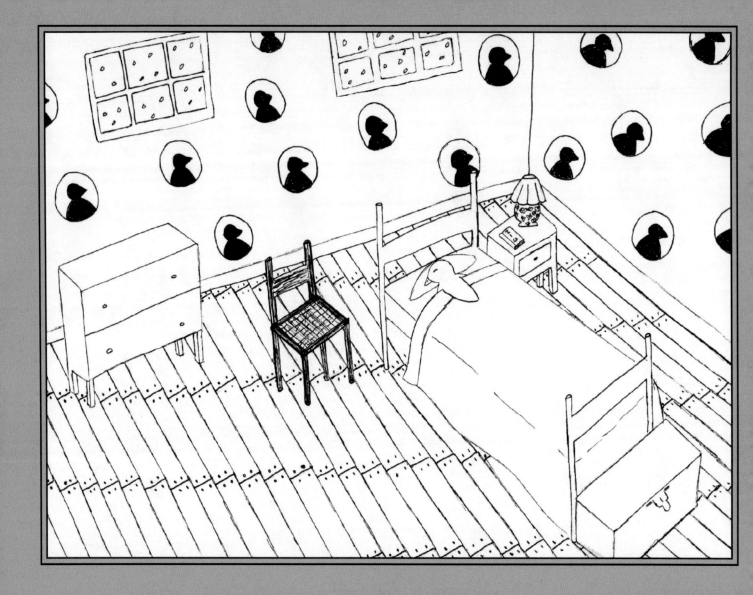

Mama Bird made Nikki practice every day until finally Nikki soared up, up and away!
Nikki soared higher than all the other birds since she had practiced the most yet happy
and excited as she was, she never started to boast.

Finally when she was tucked up in bed, exhausted after her successful flight, Mama Bird
kissed her high on her head and said, "I'm proud of you my Nikki, goodnight."

OLLY
OWL

Olly the owl always spoke his mind, he shared his ideas all of the time. He made people laugh, he made people think, he taught other owls to open their beaks.

He hooted all day and he hooted all night, he hooted the most whenever he took flight. He taught other owls to hoot when they could and hoot when they can and hoot when they should.

Sometimes he hooted to make others smile, sometimes he hooted for a really long while. He hooted when he was mad and hooted when he was sad but the biggest hoots of all came when he was glad.

Be like Olly Owl and remember to speak your mind, share your dreams with the world all of the time. Never lose faith in your voice and your mind but whenever you hoot, be like Olly, be kind.

NORMAL

Normal is normal, it's a relative word. In some places normal tigers carry normal swords. In some places it's normal for giraffes to read books to elephants that eat spaghetti inside of little nooks.

Normal is mice that dance under trees, normal is a birthday party thrown by chimpanzees. Normal is monkeys that paint their toes, normal is pigs in band playing oboes.

In some places it's normal to see flying sheep and dogs driving fast in sports cars that go "BEEP!"

To be normal
remember to always
be yourself, normal
isn't being just like
everyone else.

BRAVE DOG

Brave Dog always followed his heart, it always told him the best place to start. He didn't listen to you can'ts and you won'ts, he didn't listen to do its and don'ts.

Brave Dog wasn't a super hero, he was just like me and you, every day he imagined new things and every day they came true.

So don't forget to imagine new things, don't forget to wonder. Never lose faith in your ability to dream, even if you have a blunder. Never let people say it's not real, if it's real in your heart it can be. Keep your mind wide open and have an imagination as vast as the sea.

I love you more than the moon loves the skies, I love you more than I love apple pies.

I love you more than boats at sea, I love you more than the birds love the bees.

I love you more than I love cake, I love you more than everything Mom bakes.

I love you more than I love my car, I love you more than every shooting star.

I love you more than a tree in the fall, I love you more than my favorite ball.

I love you more than when cows moo, I love you more than I love the zoo.

I love every single thing that you do, I love you the most because you are YOU!

There are stories here, there are stories there, there are tales of mystical creatures that take place everywhere. Sometimes they make sense and sometimes they don't, sometimes they'll rhyme and sometimes they won't.

There are tales in your hometown, there are tales in far away lands, there are stories of chipmunks dancing and pigs who play in bands.

No matter what you may read, no matter what you may write, no matter what you may dream of, no matter the sheep that take flight. Remember to dream your own dreams, remember to write what you write, remember to choose your own path in this beautiful story called LIFE.

In loving memory of Paul Danziger